Home
Is a
Window

Stephanie Parsley Ledyard

Illustrations by
Chris Sasaki

NEAL PORTER BOOKS
HOLIDAY HOUSE / NEW YORK

For Aaron —S.P.L.

To Grandpa Chilly —C.S.

$18.99

Neal Porter Books

Text copyright © 2019 by Stephanie Parsley Ledyard
Illustrations copyright © 2019 by Chris Sasaki
All Rights Reserved
HOLIDAY HOUSE is registered in the U.S. Patent and Trademark Office.
Printed and bound in October 2018 at Toppan Leefung, DongGuan City, China.
The artwork for this book was made using digital tools.
Book design by Jennifer Browne
www.holidayhouse.com
First Edition
3   5   7   9   10   8   6   4   2

Library of Congress Cataloging-in-Publication Data

Names: Ledyard, Stephanie Parsley, author. | Sasaki, Chris (Illustrator), illustrator.
Title: Home is a window / Stephanie Parsley Ledyard ; illustrations by Chris Sasaki.
Description: First edition. | New York : Neal Porter Books ; Holiday House,
[2019] | Summary: "A family learns what home really means when they leave
their beloved house and move to another"-- Provided by publisher.
Identifiers: LCCN 2018009005 | ISBN 9780823441563 (hardcover)
Subjects: | CYAC: Home--Fiction. | Moving, Household--Fiction. | Family life--Fiction.
Classification: LCC PZ7.1.L39486 Hom 2019 | DDC [E]--dc23 LC record
available at https://lccn.loc.gov/2018009005

Home is a window,
a doorway,
a rug,
a basket for your shoes.

Home is
Hello, sweet pea,
and a hug,

a little bit of green,
a corner, and a chair.

Home is a table
with something good
and the people gathered there.

Home is washing,
rinsing, and drying,

and whenever a dish gets broken,
someone to help you sweep.

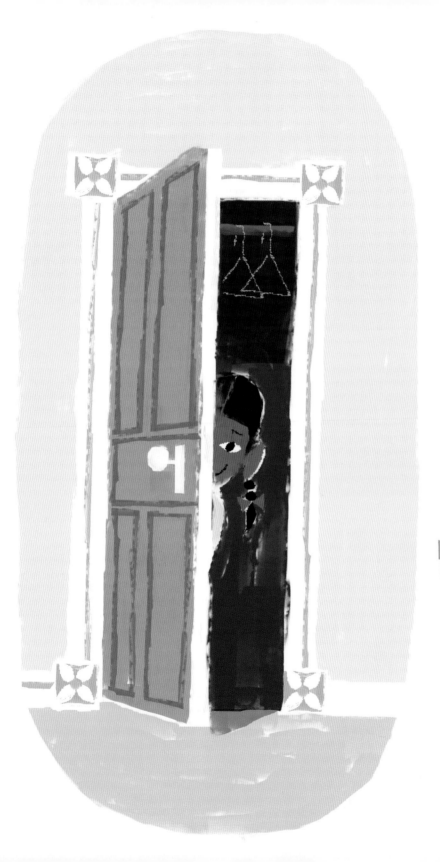

Home is one more
hide-and-seek
before bath,

bubbles
if you are lucky,

and a blanket all your own—

mostly.

Home is Ms. Vera's lamplight
shared with you,

a book before you fall asleep,

and a kiss
afterward.

Home is what feels
the same each day

and sometimes
what is new.

Home is a pillow,
the long quiet at the start of a journey,

and an arm around you tight.

Home is the shirt that
smells like your old room,

stories you had never heard,

and every song you know

sung out loud . . .

again.

Home is all that you miss

and not knowing for sure how things will be.

And then—
Here we are.

A doorway.

Hello?

A window,
sunlight,
a corner
for your toys.

A patched-up quilt,
something good,
and the people gathered near . . .

HOME.